THE SCHOOL PLAY

BY GINA AND MERCER MAYER

To Zeb with love

🔖 A GOLDEN BOOK • NEW YORK

Golden Books Publishing Company, Inc., New York, New York 10106

My teacher said, "We're going to put on a school play, and all your families will be invited." I thought that sounded cool.

My teacher gave us our parts. I was supposed to say, "Welcome to our forest. The trees are happy to see you."

When I got home I told Mom and Dad about
the play. They said they couldn't wait to see it.

Mom made my costume. I was a green elf.
I felt sort of silly. At least I didn't have to be
a sunflower.

I practiced my lines for the play every day.
I practiced in the bathtub.

I practiced for my
baby brother.

I practiced for
my sister.

I even practiced for my dog.
He got my paper and chewed it up.

At school we practiced our parts when we were supposed to be having math. That was neat.

When the night of the play came, I put on my costume. We all went to school—even my baby brother. Mom promised to keep him quiet so he wouldn't ruin the play.

My family sat in the audience. I got to go up onstage. I felt so important.

Then, while the principal was talking, I looked out from behind the curtain.

I didn't know so many people were coming.

My tummy started hurting. My teacher said it was just a little case of stage fright.

But when the curtain came up and the play started,
my tummy didn't stop hurting.

First the sunflower said his part really loud, just the way the teacher told us.

Then it was my turn.

The audience was very quiet.
Everyone was waiting for me to
say my part. I was so scared,
I couldn't remember
what to say.

Then I heard my baby brother in the audience saying, "Crido, Crido." That's what he calls me.

And everyone laughed. Then I remembered my part and I said it really loud.

I felt proud because I did a good job.
No one even knew I almost forgot.

Now that the school play is over, I guess it wasn't so bad. I don't think I'll be so scared next time.

I'll just have to make sure my baby brother sits in the front row!